This book belongs to

_____

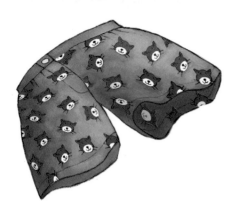

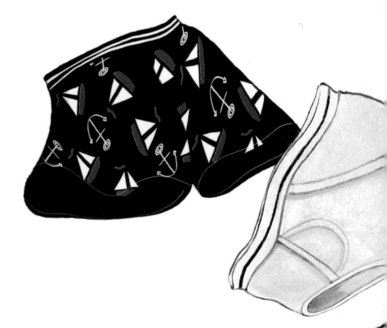
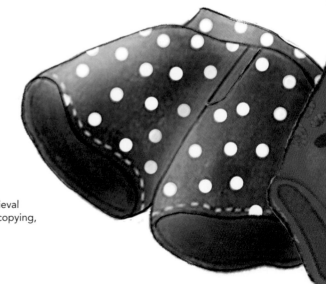

Written by Peter Bently

Illustrated by Deborah Melmon

This edition published by Parragon Books Ltd in 2014

Parragon Books Ltd
Chartist House
15–17 Trim Street
Bath BA1 1HA, UK
www.parragon.com

ISBN 978-1-4723-7721-0

Printed in China

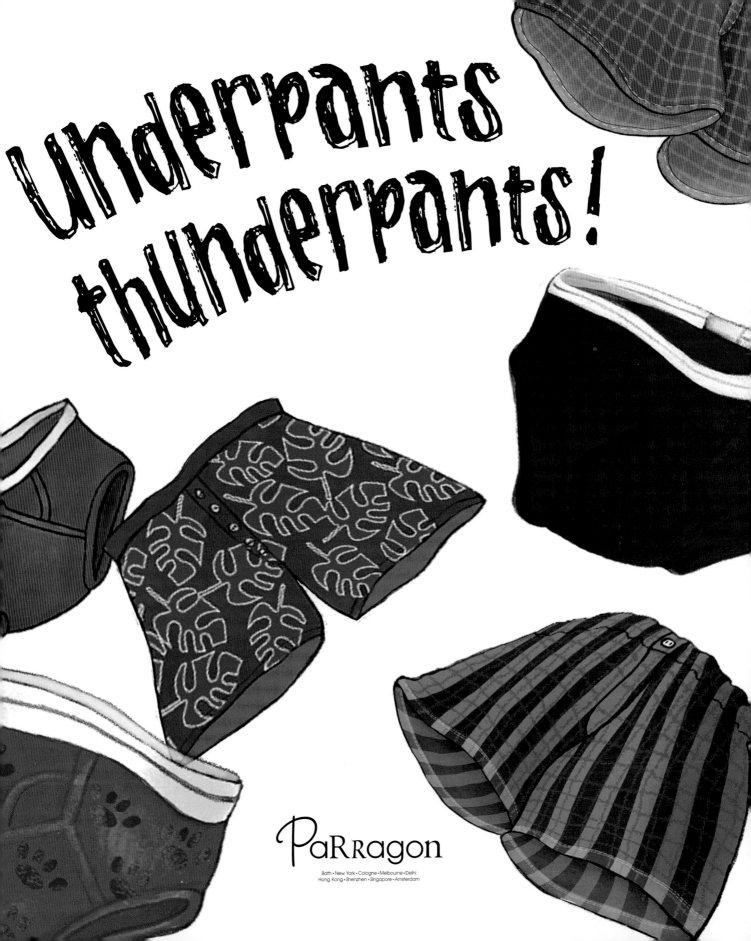

underpants thunderpants!

PaRRagon

Bath · New York · Cologne · Melbourne · Delhi
Hong Kong · Shenzhen · Singapore · Amsterdam

One day
when the weather is
sunny and **fine**,
Dog hangs his
underpants
out on the line.

But **thunder** and **lightning**
soon fill up the sky.
**underpants
thunderpants!**
Look at them
fly!

Over the **ocean**, the **jungle** and **town** – where will those **undies** come fluttering down?

"How odd," says the submarine captain below.

"First I saw **lightning** and now I see **snow!**"

hello!

Down in the **sea**
not far from the beach,
"A **giant!**
A **giant!**"
the little fish
screech.

Octopus **wriggles** and **jiggles** with **glee**.

"**Four** pairs of **underpants** perfect for me!"

Underpants plunderpants!

Just imagine that!

Roger the Pirate has got a new hat!

Safe out of sight of the **croc's** hungry eyes, Monkey's discovered a **cunning** disguise!

Elephant's **trunk** has been **tickled** by bees. *"Oh bother,"* he grumbles. "I'm going to **sneeze**, but I don't have a tissue. **What** shall I do?"

"A **JUMBO-SIZED**
hankie!
How handy! –
ATCHOO!"

Up at the **palace**, the **King** says, "**Oh my!** **Three** pairs of **underpants** baked in a pie!"

A **two-headed** alien
stares from
his **lair**...

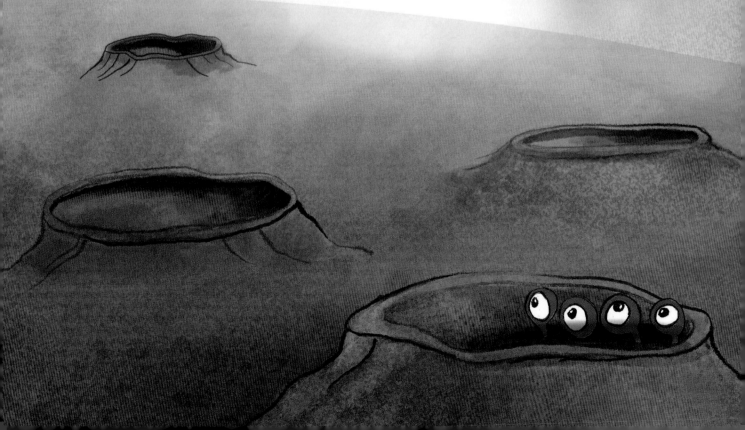

"underpants
wonderpants!
Now I'm
not **bare!**"

The
end